WHY DOESN'T HE HE LOVE ME?

Story written by author Andreya Renee

BOOK 1

WHY DOESN'T HE LOVE ME
(Book 1)

written by
Andreya Renee

Published by BlackGold Publishing, LLC in partnership with The BlackGold Book League of Hampton Roads.

1706 Todds Lane, Suite 258
Hampton, VA 23666

Edited and Formatted by: Jamel H.
Designed by: J. Matthews
First Edition: April 2025
Printed in the United States of America

PREFACE

"Boom! Boom!" I awoke with beads of salty sweat running down my face. Every night at 9:30, I would have the same nightmare. No matter how many years went by, it came back to haunt me. It was the night I met the devil who hijacked my life. I was only eighteen. That damn little sister of mine is the reason I even met him. If she had left me alone, I would have been home reading my novel.

Every day my mother would say she wished I looked like Keyshawn, and I was cursed with the look of my great-grandmother. I heard my mother say I was dark and dumb like a monkey. I never felt like I deserved to be loved by anyone. Keyshawn was built like a grown woman. Her copper complexion made her fudgy chocolate eyes stand out, and she had wavy textured hair. Mine, on the other hand, was short and what some consider nappy. I often heard, "Your sister is beautiful," while I was told, "pretty for a dark-skinned girl." I was glad when this Saturday came around because it was Horror Movie Marathon Week. Saturday nights with my caramel-flavored popcorn, Coca-Cola 16 oz, tweezer candy, pink jumbo hair rollers, avocado face mask, and pajamas. I felt like a five-year-old whenever I wore my pink fluffy bunny slippers. They were the only gift I remember getting from my mother. Sad, huh?

Keyshawn had the nerve to interrupt my movie time, talking about wanting to go to some party.

"What do you want? This is my movie night!" I couldn't believe what she had on: a white tank top with the tops of her breasts spilling out, and skinny jeans so tight they had ripples like potato chips indented in them.

"You act like the television is your man. Can't find a man cooped up in the house! And you can't screw the television! Live a little!" Look who's talking. She wants to talk about screwing when she's an open target for men to come fuck her. Against my better judgment, I decided to go and almost fainted when I saw the crowd outside a house that looked like a crack house.

"Have you lost your mind, Keyshawn?" I asked her.

"Live a little! Acting like you're too good for your own people. I'm going inside, so are you coming or not?" Keyshawn responded. The moment we stepped foot on the sidewalk, the spotlight was aimed at Keyshawn.

"Hey, baby girl, you got a man?" asked one of the male bystanders. Keyshawn blew him a kiss and kept walking while I was ignored. Being around crowds, dark lighting, and that disrespectful rap music did not sit well with me. I was more of an Anita Baker, Stephanie Mills, Mary J. Blige, and Fantasia type of girl. While Keyshawn and I were talking, a guy came up to us who happened to be our childhood friend named Terrell. Keyshawn started making out with him like I wasn't even standing there. Keyshawn stopped kissing him for a moment and turned her attention to me. Between girls twerking, grinding, and cucumber challenge songs, I felt sick to my stomach.

"So, I ain't babysitting you all night. You need to entertain yourself." She skipped her ass down the hall with him, and I decided to sit on the couch. Everybody moved away from me like I was contagious, but I also knew they didn't want to talk to the uninvited fat girl. The one guy who tried talking to her could pass for Flavor Flav from the group Public Enemy, and his breath was laced with a strong scent of weed – just like Flavor Flav. I rolled my eyes.

"Why are you sitting by yourself?" he asked.

"This isn't my type of environment," I replied. The

man took a long puff from his joint and looked at me.

"What do you mean? You ain't never visited the hood before? Apparently, the girl you came with feels right at home here. I should take a shot at her," he replied.

"There's no way in hell you are going near my sister. And yes, she's what I call a hood baby, but I prefer the finer things in life."

"So, you're a bougie bitch. I don't want you anyway. I was doing you a favor by talking to you. Nobody here checking for a fat bitch like Lizzo."

"And nobody's checking for a Flavor Flav look-alike from the group Public Enemy." I went looking for Keyshawn and found her stank ass fucking Terrell in the back bedroom. I gave her ten minutes to get dressed, or I was gonna drag her out myself.

"You're a party pooper," Keyshawn yelled at me.

"I don't care, Keyshawn. We are leaving!" Keyshawn pushed past me and headed out to the car, becoming pissed when she realized the door wouldn't open.

"Open the damn door, Kimberly!"

"Don't be yelling at me! The car ain't going nowhere. I'll be over in a minute." Several minutes after I started driving, Keyshawn decided she was going to throw a tantrum.

" Kimberly, what's your problem? I was having fun. You should try it sometime."

"Keyshawn, if fucking is your way of having fun, I want nothing to do with it."

"Whatever, Kimberly! You need some dick in your life." Seconds later, Keyshawn was holding her stomach as if she was going to get sick.

"What's wrong, Keyshawn?"

"I think I'm going to throw up." I drove nearly 70 mph to get to the nearest gas station because nobody was gonna get sick in my Beetle. Once we got to the gas station, Keyshawn bolted out of the car door and ran into the store.

"POW! POW!" I ran into the store without thinking

to find the man I saw earlier in a pool of blood with his gun next to him. Initially, I thought it was the owner who had shot him, but I saw his emerald eyes peeping out from behind the counter. There was another man who had the gun that I thought was part of the robbery too. He was nearly 6'3", a right mixture of toffee complexion, deep voice like Barry White, and weighed nearly 200 pounds. Had me singing "When We" by Tank in my head. Within seconds, I felt like I was tackled by Keyshawn. When the cops questioned the Indian owner and Keyshawn, I felt a certain way and noticed the cops treated the unfamiliar man like he was one of them.

"Be nice. He saved your life. Do you not think he would be locked up if he was?" She poked her lips out and crossed both her arms. She scanned him up and down with a Pitbull mug on her face.

"I saw you talking to those cops. Seemed like your buddies while they treated the owner and I like criminals. I don't like pigs, and you might as well be one of them. You're still black with that high yellow skin tone of yours."

"You would be **dead**..."

"Arrogant asshole," Keyshawn said. I had to take care of this conversation before things got out of hand, and this man had steam coming out of his ears like a mad bull.

"Forgive my sister for her attitude. Thank you for saving her." Keyshawn rolled her eyes and took off when she claimed to see someone across the street.

"I did not get your name. My name is Kimberly."

"My name is Charlie." I nearly fainted when he took my hand and kissed it. His eyes were burning into my soul, and he was undressing me with his eyes. We stared at each other for a moment and felt electricity between us. Those pearly white teeth made me warm on the inside.

"I would like to take you on a date," Charlie said.

"Sir, it is nice talking to you..." I began.
"But I am **not** interested."

CHAPTER ONE
CHARLIE

As I stood at the door of the gas station, I couldn't shake the feeling that things were about to go sideways. I had no intention of getting caught, but bringing a junkie along was a mistake. When the situation turned chaotic, I had to take control. Killing the crackhead was my only option, and I threatened the cashier to keep quiet.

Back at home, I hoped for some peace. As I approached the door, I heard the joyful singing of my kids watching "The Little Mermaid." The moment I stepped inside, they rushed towards me with excitement.

"Daddy! Daddy," they cried. My oldest, Imani, was five, and my youngest, Mint (Emily), was three. Imani, with her sharp ears and curious nature, was always in the know.

"Momma said you were on the six o'clock news," Imani blurted out.

"Brenda, why are they watching that stuff?" I snapped. "Poisoning their minds."

"They overheard me on the phone. But it doesn't change the fact that you were on the news, part of a robbery?"

"Let's not discuss it in front of the kids," I said, leading Brenda to our bedroom.

"What the hell, Charlie? What happened this time? I told you to be careful. Stop picking up crackheads to help you."

"I thought I had it under control until..."

"Until *what*?"

"Never mind. Look, he's dead, and no one will think I did it. They'll pin it on him."

"I just wish you'd find another profession," she said.

"Don't worry. This is temporary. I might have a job opportunity coming up."

"I hope so."

Minutes later, the kids' laughter filled the living room. "Let's see what these daredevils are up to."

Days after the incident, I got a call from my godfather.

"Hello, son. I saw you on the news. Are you okay? Brenda must've been angry."

"That's an understatement. But why did you call?"

"I need a favor. Do you remember my daughter?"

Immediately, I thought of Keyshawn, a known troublemaker. "The wild one?" I asked.

"No, the other one," he clarified. I recalled her vaguely from a party where she disrupted my plans.

"What kind of favor?"

"I need you to marry her."

I was stunned. He knew I had a family, and Brenda was the only woman I intended to marry. "Are you nuts? I have Brenda, and she would—"

"I know. But money can make people think differently. I'll give you and Brenda one million dollars to buy the house she's always wanted. Trust me, the money will change her mind."

That night, I discussed it with Brenda. As expected, she was furious at first. But when I mentioned the money and the house, her tone changed.

CHAPTER TWO
KIMBERLY

Two weeks later, I went grocery shopping at a local Walmart when I bumped into another shopping cart.

"I'm so sorr..." Before I could finish what I was saying, I noticed it was the man named Charlie from the gas station robbery.

"Are you *following* me?" I asked him.

"No," he chuckled. When I looked in his shopping cart, I saw nothing but rabbit food and organic items, which made me think he was a health nut.

"You don't eat meat?" I asked.

"I do, but I also eat healthy. If you let me take you out, you'll see I have a well-rounded taste."

Keyshawn thought it was a bad idea, but for some reason, my parents seemed elated. I remember it like it was yesterday. He agreed to pick me up at 7:30 PM from my parents' house. I chose a red body-con dress that showed off every inch of my body. Keyshawn did my makeup and hair, which she was good at. He arrived in his black Mercedes-Benz looking like a model for a tuxedo company.

"Hello there, beautiful," he said. I couldn't stop blushing. He was a true gentleman and opened my door for me. "Isn't She Lovely" by Stevie Wonder blasted out of the speakers. He put a blindfold on me and said he wanted to take me somewhere special. It seemed like forever before he shut off the engine. When I got out, the cold feel of sand was beneath my feet, and the taste of saltwater clashed in the distance. Several minutes later, he took off my blindfold, and my eyes almost popped out of my head when I saw where we were. He had taken me to Cumberland Island, with candles lining our walkway. At the end, there was a beautifully decorated table with a waiter standing next to it. I felt like I was on cloud nine, being treated like a true queen.

"You did this for *me*?" I asked.

"You deserve the best," he replied. He checked off every box in my book for being a gentleman. Even the waitress blushed a little. I felt as if I was on cloud nine and had found a potential mate. After we had settled in our seats, Charlie started talking.

"So, tell me about yourself," he asked.

"Well, there isn't much to tell. I'm eighteen, have a younger sister named Keyshawn who you already met. I stay at home and plan on going to film school next year."

"That's amazing. You could be the next Shonda Rhimes. I love someone who's got something of their own going on."

"How about yourself? Like you getting caught in the middle of a robbery," I responded.

"At the wrong place at the wrong time. Mother always said I stood up for the underdog. Enough about how we met; I want to focus on the present," he said.

"Sounds good to me. Speaking of the present, what do you feel about gender roles in a relationship?" I asked.

"I believe it's 50/50. Problems at home?" he asked.

"I wouldn't say that. My father is a tyrant, my mother is a doormat, and my sister is a bitch."

"I would treat you like a queen if you were with **me**."

When we arrived back at my parents' house, I believed I had found the one. Keyshawn's nosy self was still up when I came back from the date.

"How was the date with the pig?" She flopped down on the bed with a bag of bacon-flavored popcorn.

"It was amazing!"

"Momma and Drill Sergeant Daddy are talking about you and your pig date. They're saying you're going to marry that pig. I don't know what you see in him."

"I could say the same thing about you and Terrell. He's a wannabe thug, but you still mess with him." Keyshawn's face twisted, and she stopped eating her popcorn.

"Terrell ain't no stranger or pig! Has it ever crossed your mind that Donovan has a thing for you? He looks like a nerd, but at least you know him." Here we go with this Donovan nonsense. I knew Donovan had eyes for me, but I needed someone new to be involved with. Somebody that didn't know my baggage.

"Donovan is busy doing him. You don't see him calling me, do you? So zip it about Donovan."

"So be it. You'll regret it when somebody else grabs Donovan. You're better off with him." Keyshawn needed to mind her business and worry about getting STDs from Terrell. Charlie took me to the Fox Theatre several weeks later to see The Lion King. He was a true gentleman the entire night, and he made my heart melt on the inside.

Three Months Later

This was my wedding day, and the little girl inside me was jumping up and down with joy. When I looked in the mirror, I saw a black Barbie doll draped in a pearl white lace dress with a train behind her. The white color made my dark chocolate complexion stand out, showcasing the curvy shape I was once ashamed to embrace. I wished my father would have walked me down the aisle, but he was away on a business trip. Instead, a male family member agreed to walk me down the aisle. My mother opted not to attend the wedding because she never went anywhere without my father. Keyshawn didn't agree with it, but she was there to support me because neither of our parents was there. While my male family member walked me down the aisle, he questioned what I was doing.

"Baby girl, you sure about this?"

"My father is not here to walk me down the aisle, nor is my mother."

"Baby girl, you can't make decisions based on others' feelings. Your father is a stubborn pit bull, and your mother always follows his lead. Do you want to do this?"

"I *love* him."

"That's all that matters." He walked back to his seat, putting holes in the picture of the man I was about to marry. I wondered, what did I really know about Charlie? Was I making a mistake? I thought I was the happiest woman alive on my wedding day, but a small voice in my head asked, "Do you really want to do this?" I couldn't deny the red flags I saw with Charlie, but I thought I could overlook them when we got married. One occasion stood out during our short engagement. We had gone to dinner on a beautiful Sunday afternoon with the sun shining down on us, giving me false hope that everything would go smoothly. Rookery was like a second kitchen because we were always there, and I couldn't cook. While we were at the table, a bombshell blonde waitress with chalk-white complexion, forest green contacts, and a soda-bottle shape came to our table. "How may I help you?" she spoke with a mouse-like voice. Charlie, an alpha male, always spoke for both of us.

"Blueberry cobbler shake, two classic city cheeseburgers, and a vanilla shake." Charlie threw the menu at her like she was the school janitor. Charlie was a full-grown kid who never liked hearing the word no. I was used to his tantrums at this point. The waitress's hand trembled.

"Sir, we're out of blueberry cobbler shake. We can give you another flavor. Fruity Pebbles tastes pretty good." The air was sucked out of the room, and I saw Charlie's wrist begin to curl up at the table. His eyes became dangerously large, his body tensing up like a stone statue. I thought I would shield her from the outburst.

"Sure, we will take another..." Before I could finish, I saw the anger in his eyes. I knew I had spoken out of turn in his mind, and he gave me a "shut the fuck up" look. Charlie suddenly went mute. Everything on the table was demolished, and the waitress ran to the back. Charlie started demanding what he wanted and raising hell in the restaurant. Two other male employees restrained him until the police came and locked him in the back of a police car, screaming at the window. As I got up, I could feel people beaming their eyes at my neck and whispering among themselves, bringing back memories of my father's public outbursts during my childhood. One incident stood out the **most**. I was eleven at the time when the waiter came to our table. My father always ordered first, then Keyshawn, my mother, and lastly me. On this occasion, there wasn't any chicken, and he raised hell like Charlie did. As a result, my father was arrested and took the car keys with him. My mother, sister, and I had to walk three miles' home. It was a memory I would never forget.

"DING! DONG!" The alarm clock went off, and I started getting dressed to go down to the police station, feeling like I had done something wrong myself. The police station was filled with lunatics, hoes, and criminals. All I could smell was smoke and alcohol. He came out walking past me, and I had to run to keep up with him. I was almost out of breath when I caught up.

"*Where the fuck have you been*!?" He got himself locked up, not me.

"How are you gonna get an attitude with me? You put yourself there. I was home in my bed." Charlie hit me so hard I stumbled back several feet, hitting a streetlight pole, with Looney Tunes circles going around my head and a river of blood from my nose. I felt like I broke my back, and everything went black. Charlie squatted down next to me with those devil eyes. "Don't you ever talk back to me. Bring your black ass on." On another occasion, Charlie and I were having one of our arguments, and he left me standing at the gas station alone.

I walked inside to get some cigarettes, and that's when I bumped into someone from the past.

"Kimmie?" he asked. I couldn't believe Donovan was standing in front of me, looking the same as he did when we were young teenagers. I felt ashamed to be standing there alone with my wedding ring glistening with diamonds, bouncing off the sunlight through the window.

"I see you're married," he said. "How long if you don't mind me asking?"

"Two years so far. I didn't know you were back in town."

"Just visiting my mother. Did you walk here? I don't see any cars outside." I didn't want to tell him the truth, but someone else in the store decided to spill my tea.

"Her man left her stranded outside and sped off like a madman," said another customer. I wanted to shove that blueberry Slurpee down her throat. She should mind her business because her man looked like he was high on weed.

"Is that true?" Donovan asked.

"You don't see any man, do you?" asked the same customer.

"Bitch, shut the fuck up! Leave them be," said the man with her. I was glad that she left the store, but the truth was exposed to Donovan.

"There's no judgment from me. I don't mind giving you a ride home." Against better judgment, I accepted his offer, knowing the moment I did, I entered dangerous territory.

"Your husband doesn't deserve you." I ignored what he said and started playing with the radio. Several minutes later, I felt his manly hand rubbing against my thigh, sending an electric shock up my body. He told me he was taking me home, but he passed the exit to my house and went into the park instead.

"I asked you to take me home, not here." He acted like he didn't hear what I said.

"Don't act like you don't remember when we used to come here and have fun. I know you felt the sexual energy between us. You really think your husband loves you like I do. I thought we had plans of being together, but you ran off to be with a man you barely know." Donovan had some nerve to get in his feelings when he was the one who acted like I was nothing to him. Donovan and I weren't on speaking terms when I met Charlie because of Donovan's behavior.

"Really, Donovan? You want to act like we were on good terms at the time. You had plenty of chances to say something before I married him."

"You really don't know the man you're married to," he replied. It took my breath away for a moment because he had never met my husband, Charlie.

"You're just being a jealous ex." Donovan got quiet for a moment, which meant there was something else on his mind.

"Apparently, you don't know this, but your husband has some screws loose in his head. That jackass somehow found me to talk about you. He threatened to chop off my dick and gave me Charles Manson vibes. I don't mess with crazy people."

"He wouldn't do that." Without warning, Donovan kissed me, and I didn't push him away. When I arrived home and opened the door, the living room light came on, and Charlie was sitting in his favorite chair with a cigar in his mouth.

"Where did you go with that man?"

"You left me stranded, and he was an old friend who brought me home."

"Lying bitch!" He got up and came over to where I was standing and sniffed my clothes. He blew smoke in my face before he spoke again. "I can smell him on you. You're out here being a whore while my wife. Embarrassing me in public and saying fuck you to my face. I can send you back to where I found you, where nobody cared about you." Several weeks later, I got a reminder of what I did with Donovan. Without saying a word, it seemed like Charlie already knew.

"You're pregnant with the bastard's baby, aren't you? I haven't touched you, that's for **sure**."

CHAPTER THREE
KIMBERLY

Present Day
ATLANTA GEORGIA

I was recommended a new therapist after a breakdown at the library. Instead of returning to my old therapist, I decided to see someone new. Every Monday morning at 9 a.m., I would visit Sherry. She was 5'6" with a toffee-brown complexion and freckles that covered her face. Some people said she looked like Nia Long. Her hair was styled in a sleek, black bob.

"Good morning, Kimberly. I am happy to see you today," Sherry said, directing me to the couch. Minutes later, she had me look at myself in the mirror, even though I dreaded the reflection.

Being fat, Black, and feeling undesirable seemed like a curse. "What the hell happened to us?" I thought to myself. Joy no longer looked back at me in the mirror, but sadness did. I knew I was desired by other men; my husband was not one of them. Looking in the mirror triggered a flashback.

On my wedding night, I stood in front of a mirror, thrilled to be married to the man of my dreams. Every day, I woke up to love letters and my favorite candy. Sometimes, he would dance silly for me. This morning, I woke to the scent of Charlie next to me, which made me smile inside.

"Baby, good morning," said Charlie, coming into the room smelling like sweet cinnamon rolls with breakfast cooked for me.

"You are so sweet, honey." Despite the gesture, I couldn't shake the thought of my 30-pound weight gain. I wondered if he had noticed. He must have, because he stopped and looked at me for a moment.

"*What's wrong, honey?*"

"I've gained weight."

"You're beautiful, Kimberly. No matter how much you change, I'll always love you."

Sherry's voice brought me back to the present. "What do you see?" she asked. When I looked in the mirror, I saw an hourglass shape turned into a jug, relaxed hair turned into a bush, and a woman who used to dress sexy now dressed like a grandma. I could see why he was no longer attracted to me. Why doesn't he love me? I asked myself.

"I do not know. I feel useless to him because I cannot bear children. It feels like I am his maid instead of his wife. Just there to keep the image."

"Don't say that! A woman's sole purpose is not to be barefoot and pregnant. This ain't the 1950s. You ain't less of a woman because you can't bear any more children. Is a man less of a man because he gets a snip downstairs? Nope! And neither are we. Let me be real with you: Get rid of that no-good piece of shit you call a husband. What do you see in him?"

"I love him. He's the only man in my life who showed me attention and affection."

"How's your relationship with your father, if I may ask?" Sherry inquired.

"More like non-existent. I always felt like I was something that should've never been born. I was always the unlovable one, and nobody blinked an eye at me."

"Tell me about your upbringing. Was it a happy one?"

"My father was a tyrant, and my mother was a doormat. He made my mom, sister, and I walk behind him whenever we went somewhere together. I never understood why."

"You got mommy and daddy issues. You need to see yourself in a positive light. You have a daughter to think about. Look in the mirror and think about when you were your daughter's age. What did your younger self feel about herself?"

"The little girl who never got love from her mother or father. Just unwanted by anyone."

"Has it ever dawned on you that your daughter sees the same thing when she looks in the mirror?" It hadn't dawned on me until she said it.

"I want you to practice self-love and show your daughter what unconditional love looks like. Do something that makes you happy, like indie filmmaking. Your daughter needs that element. I guarantee she will be happy to see her mother in a happy place. Meet new people and see new things." It had crossed my mind a few times, but I never had the courage to go. But I immediately thought about the upcoming indie film meetup at the library.

When I arrived back home, I saw Sara on the couch reading a book and went over to kiss her on the forehead. She looked at me strangely.

"Something wrong, Mommy?" she asked.

"Nope. Just wanted to kiss you on the forehead and say I love you." As I walked towards the bathroom to take a shower, I glanced back at Sara and saw a smile on her face.

After my shower, I prepared dinner. Every day, I felt the air was sucked out of the room whenever Charlie came home from work. He worked at the church as a minister, which required long hours and made him very salty when he came home. I always washed clothes on Thursday, as designated by Charlie. This Thursday, my stomach twisted and turned. As I picked up the dirty clothes off the floor, one of Charlie's white shirts fell out. When I bent down, I thought the stain on it was a paint mark or highlighter.

My heart sank when I examined it further. It was cupid-shaped lipstick, bubblegum pink. "These are not mine. I have full lips, and I would never wear that color," I said to myself. I began to wonder if all those times Charlie came home late smelling like roses, he was with the bubblegum pink lip girl. Dread filled my heart because my marriage was crumbling before my eyes. I took the shirt into the kitchen to find some lighter fluid and matches. I walked out onto the porch, which creaked every time somebody walked on it.

The steps down the porch were literally falling apart, with one step missing. I almost fell when I stepped on the ground because the grass was wet and mushy like mashed potatoes. I walked around the porch and threw the shirt in a rusty barrel, which became engulfed in flames when I lit the fire. As I watched the flames die out, I was disturbed by Mrs. Wineo. She always had an opinion about something.

"What are you doing?"

"Burning stuff." She eyeballed me oddly with a hand on her hip, thinking I was lying.

"Where's your husband?"

"Away on business."

"He's always away on business. Only see him once a month, honestly. What kind of man is that? My beloved husband, God bless his soul, never had me doing heavy lifting. Calls himself a pastor, huh. That husband of yours should be ashamed of himself." I rolled my eyes, wishing she would go away and was relieved when she did. I went inside to get a glass of wine. I knew from experience Charlie would not try to explain the lipstick mark; he would simply blow me off. Charlie arrived home several hours later in a grumpy mood. Suddenly, he came out of the bedroom like a mad bull and knocked my drink out of my hand.

"Where's my white shirt?"

"I do not know."

"Bitch, I know you destroyed it. Next time my stuff ends up missing, so will you." Charlie spit in my face. "Clean that shit on the floor. You better have something on the dinner table when I come back." I sat as a robot, without flinching while Charlie spoke to me. He stormed out, leaving my heart broken to pieces. Insult to injury, he did not come back, and Sara gave me a questioning look. My heart broke when I read the words Sara wrote in her diary after Charlie left. It was hard to read, but it was something I needed to know. I remember what my therapist told me about breaking generational curses and breaking them before it is too late. I found her diary and started reading it.

Dear Diary, Aug. 30, 2015

I wish momma showed me love more often. She's terrified of Charlie. She doesn't know how he treats me when she isn't around. Calls me a slut or a nosy bitch. Always gives me hateful looks. I wish my mom would choose my well-being over his. I know he's not my real father. I'm a ghost to him, and my mom doesn't know how to love me. I just want my mom to show her love towards me more often or say I love you.

      I never imagined Sara had these thoughts. I knew that Charlie and Sara did not talk to each other much, but I never thought it was like that. I went outside to find Sara sitting underneath the oak tree. The moment I laid eyes on her brown eyes in the delivery room, I fell in love with her. On the other hand, when I looked at her hair, it reminded me of the nature of her birth.

Even though Charlie said he would support me throughout my pregnancy, his actions said otherwise. I gave birth to my baby girl in a room absent of my husband and surrounded by a room full of nurses and doctors who treated me like family. Charlie showed up several hours later with a sour look on his face. As she grew up, we would go to the park every weekend to spend time together.

Now she had a terrified look on her face, and I realized I had become like my own mother.

"Am I in trouble?" she asked. When I looked in her eyes, I saw myself looking back at me when I was her age. "No. I read your diary entry…" Sara's demeanor went from terrified to wounded. She started biting her bottom lip. I lifted her face to look at me. Tear-drop tears streamed down her face.

"It is okay. It is my fault because I made you feel that way."

"Mommy, do you love me?" she asked. Without hesitation, I grabbed her and embraced her in a hug where she sobbed on my arm.

"Of course, I do. You're my baby girl. Mommy has been dealing with her own demons and putting my frustrations on you. It is not fair to you. Mommy loves you more than anything in this world and would take a bullet for you."

"Is that why he hates me because I'm not his?" she asked. I knew she was talking about Charlie, and at this moment, I wanted to beat the shit out of him.

"That has nothing to do with you. He just has issues with mommy he needs to deal with. Remember, someone's opinion of you doesn't determine who you are. From this day, I promise to be a better mother to you, regardless of whether I am if I am in this relationship or not. You are my baby girl and I love you. About we go inside and make your favorite chocolate chip cookies?" A smile came on her face which warmed my heart on the inside.

CHAPTER FOUR
KEYSHAWN

I never understood why Kimberly married that jackass, and now he's got her looking like a damn fool on TV. To make it worse, my best friend Khandish was watching with me.

"Ain't that Kimberly running in the street like a mad woman?" she chuckled. I pinched her arm, causing her to tilt the popcorn bowl. Yes, Kimberly was losing her mind, but she was my sister, and nobody else was gonna talk about her.

"Khandish…"

"Don't start that 'she's my sister' shit. You can't deny what's showing on the television. There's no way in hell I would be chasing after a man and his mistress." I shot her a glare because we both knew that was near impossible.

"Khandish, you don't like dick." Khandish was about to speak, but I cut her off. "Don't act like you haven't lost your mind over some pussy. Remember Rebecka?" Khandish avoided looking at me for a moment because that shit almost got us both killed.

"Do you have to bring that up?" she asked.

"Yeah, because you're not gonna sit here and pretend like Kimberly is the only fool for love.

Rebecka had your ass wrapped around her finger, and you almost killed another bitch because of her. Had me driving to save our lives because her crazy ass was hunting us down." Khandish pretended to choke on some popcorn but stopped when she saw me staring at her.

"Fine, Keyshawn. But at least mine loved me. And I don't cause scenes in public. No offense, but I think everyone at that church is waiting for her to explode. One of the girls I was with goes to that church and says it was an open secret."

"I mean, do they know she's a lesbian, or is that an open secret too? Look, you're my friend and all, but you've done things ten times worse in the name of love. And we BOTH could be six feet under for it. The only difference between you and Kimberly is that yours wasn't blasted on TV."

"Keyshawn, my bad. I was just telling you what the streets are saying. I'll admit I haven't had the best relationships, but you've got it better than the rest of us, straight or not."

"Khandish, what are you talking about?" I asked.

"Now you're the one pretending. Just because I prefer pussy doesn't mean I can't acknowledge a handsome man when I see one. AND Terrell is a handsome man. You ain't fucked him yet?"

"Khandish?"

"We both know you're a sex freak. You deserve a good-looking man after what you've been through. Don't let one bad apple make you miss the blessing standing right in front of you."

"Terrell is an old friend of mine." Khandish set down her bowl of popcorn and forced me to look at her.

"Does he know about what happened six years ago? I already know your family doesn't." I just shook my head no. "You should tell him, Keyshawn."

CHAPTER FIVE
CHARLIE

I f I were being honest, I never thought I would grow up to be a Pastor. Growing up, when I heard the word Pastor, I thought about the pimps on the corner. They wore the best suits with a Bible in one hand. One of them was my mother's pimp named Juicy, who taught me the game. I had a rough patch with the police, which landed me with a felony charge. When everybody else turned their backs on me, there was one person I could always go to.

"Hello, young man. I'm sorry to hear what happened to your momma. What brings you here?"

"Remember you told me about making money in the church? I need a job and am having a hard time finding one. Can you teach me how to do it?" Juicy gave me a once-over, a cigar hanging out of his mouth. He connected me with a group of traveling Pastors who were ex-cons and pimps themselves. It lasted several months, and I knew I wasn't going back to being broke. A week after the traveling gig ended, I had my eyes on the church in the neighborhood and even visited it. The Pastor looked like a dried-up prune, and whatever he said was repeated by someone behind him. I told Juicy I wanted to preach there, and he made it possible. I soon learned how money could be made by reciting scriptures I honestly didn't believe in. Every Sunday, I was the king of my household, and everyone had to obey me. The congregation praised me, thinking I cared about them. To me, all I saw was money filling my pockets.

I was heading to church as usual when Kay's friend Tianna showed up. She was ten times worse than Keyshawn. Three years ago, that tramp moved into the neighborhood and made my life a living hell. Kay and Tianna became fast friends, and she was over at my house quite a bit. I already had enough problems with that old white bitch Miss Grace, and now another bitch had moved into the neighborhood. I remember the day I first saw her. But I couldn't deny she had a fat ass and big boobs. I couldn't stop looking at her pulling those weeds. Kimberly came to stand next to me at the window.

"You're staring at Tianna now," Kay said.

"Who the hell is Tianna?" I asked. Kay pointed to the window where the woman was pulling out weeds. "How do you know her?" I asked.

"I met her at a craft show." In the back of my mind, I thought, "I gotta deal with another bitch coming over to my house." I decided to talk to my friend Samuel, whom I met at an underground poker game.

"Hey, Charlie!" yelled Samuel.

"Hello, Samuel." He was drinking moonshine on his porch, and I knew exactly what he was staring at.

"You see that new girl over there?" said Samuel.

"She's in the eye view of my kitchen window," said Charlie.

"She's a nice piece of ass. Black goddess."

"Honestly, I would fuck her, but I wouldn't claim her." Samuel almost broke his neck looking at me.

"What the fuck? She could pass for a runway model."

"She's too brown for me."

" Kimberly is..."

"That's different."

"How? Both are the same complexion and both equally beautiful."

"That's your opinion." To some men, her melanin skin would be a turn-on, but to me, it was a turn-off. Made me want to vomit. The more melanin a woman had, the more I got sick to my stomach. The only reason Kay was tolerable was because she was a good house slave—I mean housewife—and needed a good image for the church. Everybody liked black love like the Obamas, or LeBron James and his wife. But Kay had an expiration date like the food in the refrigerator.

That tramp decided to come over today. "Hey, Kimberly! I saw Miss Grace leaving." Kay was in the kitchen, and this tramp was acting like I wasn't in the living room.

"Don't know how to speak to somebody?" She rolled her eyes and popped her bubblegum in my direction.

33

"Hello, jackass! You got a staring issue?"

"Hood rat bitch!"

"True colors coming out, huh? Pastor? You ain't no better than me, hustler. Remember the girl who wore the red wig who came to church?" I played dumb with her, but how could I forget?

"Let me refresh your memory. She and her mother were evicted, and they came to you for help. Instead, you told them you needed a blowjob performed by both before you would help them. And two hundred dollars were given to keep them quiet about it." I was glad Kay called her into the kitchen to get away from me. What Tianna didn't know was that those whores sold sex for a living, and I don't do shit for free.

I left to go to church and was encountered by Rosie, the secretary. She was overweight, had "I Love Lucy" glasses, a face filled with freckles, and a raspy voice. Always cut her eyes at me whenever I walked through the door. It was no secret she didn't like me and missed the old pastor. Thought she could tell me how to be a good pastor and what the old pastor would do. She had to go! So, one day, she didn't show up for work, and everybody asked where she was.

The next day, I held interviews for a new secretary. The first one was too damn old and looked like Mr. Rogers. The second one was a male who was flamboyant. The third one had too much mouth for me. I had gone through nearly ten people, and I was on the verge of giving up. I was elated when she walked through the door, and I could tell she was happy to see me too.

"Charlie? You're a Pastor? I thought Pastor Jenkins..."

"He was, but he died several months ago. What are you doing here?"

"Job interview. Look, I don't mind being at home with our babies, but I need to be around people. And spend some time with you."

"What are you thinking? My wife is..." I said. She sat down across from me, which messed with my concentration.

"Wife? Let me remind your ass of this: You married that bitch for money only and should've annulled that marriage six months ago, but your ass is still with that bitch? I don't know why. If... let me correct myself—when I start working here, nobody's gonna think nothing. Fuck what people got to say, and they're gonna just think I'm the secretary. And I want to keep it that way." Immediately after the interview, I brought the staff together and prepared to tell them Rosie moved to Miami. I knew by their sour puss faces they were already feeling a way. When I sat down, Sister Jenny stared at me.

"As we all know, Rosie was getting older and moving to Miami to be with family," I said. The rest of the board members gave me pushback.

"What has gotten into you? First, you are praising President 45 in the sermon, and now you are talking about Rosie being gone. She's been here longer than you are alive," said Mary Marie. After she spoke, another one of the elders started speaking.

"Fuck that! Your ass is an embarrassment to God." Everyone looked at her with their mouths open and shook their heads. Lastly, they looked at me like I made her say that shit. I was glad when she excused herself from the room. After they all left the conference room, I went back to my office, where I found Brenda sitting at my desk.

"Really, CHARLIE? That sermon caused a stir in the congregation. I also saw you in the conference room with the staff. I guess they didn't like you talking in favor of President 45 and having a new secretary," she chuckled. I wanted to smack that smirk off her face, but I didn't want any smoke from her jailbird brothers.

"Brenda, I've had enough problems, and I don't need your mouth to be one of them."

"You need a chill pill, and I know what you need." Without warning, she decided to give me fellatio, which was exactly what I needed, and I was on cloud nine. It was interrupted by Kay busting through the door, and Brenda jumped up and bolted out the door. Kay was throwing things and turning her rage on me, and I was chasing after Brenda with my pants halfway down, unzipped. When I reached my car, Brenda was inside, looking like a scared little puppy.

"What the hell, Brenda? Why did you run off like that?"

"I panicked. She went crazy," she said.

"Now you see what I mean. She's lost her mind." Brenda remained quiet. "Cat got your tongue?" I asked.

"I can't believe you let this shit go this far," Brenda muttered. She had a lot of nerve being smart because she agreed to this plan from the beginning.

"Don't act like that. I'm doing this for both of us. Now you feel sorry for her?"

"Of course not! I'm your one and only wife. But we can't be in town..."

"I got it figured out already."

"And the congregation?"

"They'll believe whatever I tell them." I decided that it was best we got out of town for a little while. My grandfather bought a log cabin when he was a young man and gave it to me after he passed away since I was his only grandchild. Several hours later, we arrived at the log cabin, which surprised Brenda.

"I haven't been here since the birth of Imani. Generous gift from your grandfather. He must have been rich or something."

"Nah, he got a lump sum of money and bought this cabin with it."

I was glad when Thursday came because it was the day Samuel and I went fishing like we always do, but something was off this time. Samuel was never quiet this long, and it was getting on my nerves.

"What's up with you?" I asked. Samuel kept messing with his fishing rod for a moment before speaking.

"Do you really enjoy being a Pastor? Or are you doing it for profit?" What had gotten into him? Had someone put a bug in his ear?

"Is there something you know that I don't?" I asked. For a moment, I thought about the time he caught me talking to Juicy.

"Playing dumb now? I know you talk to Juicy. And you and I both know why. You're my best friend and all, but I gotta be real with you." It was no secret Samuel had a disdainful feeling about Juicy.

Honestly, it was none of his business, and he had no right to talk. He would use the money to pay whores to come to his house, and some of them were property of Juicy.

"What do you have against him? He's a Pastor, for God's sake."

"Lemme think. For one, he's a known pimp and being a Pastor is just a money bag to him. Didn't he date your momma when she was a stripper? But you still talk to him knowing he pimped your momma out." The thought of what my mother did made me sick to my stomach. Juicy came out of her bedroom, and I knew he had given her dope to keep her in another world for a while. This time was different because when he came out, he started talking to me.

"Hey, little man! Come take a walk with me." I was seven at the time, but I felt like a grown man taking a walk with him.

"Do you know what I do?" he asked.

"Sell women for money." He had a smirk on his face.

"Little man, I see it as a way to sell fantasies to men. But there's something else I do by managing women on the street. See that church over there?" he asked. He pointed to a church that looked like a Gothic dungeon from the 18th century. In my mind, a pimp and a church had no space in the same room together. I knew it had something to do with money.

"I know you think it's a place to help the needy, but it's also a hustle for me."

"How?"

"Little man, everybody praises you when you're a Pastor, even if you've done wrong. I could ask the congregation for ten thousand dollars for the church by the end of the week, and I would get it. There's no amount of money they won't pay to keep the house of JESUS going."

"Don't they know you are a pimp? Isn't being a pimp a sin?" Juicy gave me a stern look.

"What do you know about sin? The sin you probably see is your momma being what the church folks call sinners. Regarding me being a pimp, I see it as a business. And I have the gift of making people believe JESUS comes through. You must move into

41

whatever character you're playing at the time. You'll see when you get older."

Samuel's tapping brought me back to the present.

"You might see it that way, but she was grown and chose that. Kay reminds me of my mother." Samuel sat down next to me and looked at the photo I pulled out of my wallet. She had a beige complexion, thick curly hair, chocolate brownie-colored eyes, and full lips. "She was a hooker who everybody called Peggy. I was thirteen when I saw what she did to get money. My friend pointed her out to me. Said, 'That's your momma over there being a whore.' She was an embarrassment and kept calling me baby boy. I had enough and got rid of her." The look on Samuel's face was priceless, and I got enjoyment out of it. He wouldn't take me seriously because we were drinking.

"You killed your momma?" he asked.

"Of course not, Samuel. I meant I went to live with my father. Why do you think such a thing? We're talking about my wife, not my momma."

"Wanna talk about your wife? Fine. Since we are talking about her, that's some foul shit you did at the

42

church. You became infamous overnight. How do you think she feels about being on the news chasing after you? You might want to join the unemployment line across town." What the hell was his problem?

"Whose side are you on? I'm your friend, not her," I asked.

"True. But I gotta call you out on your bullshit. Why do you treat her so bad?"

"She's unworthy of my time and my love." Samuel shook his head.

"She's your wife. Is there something I don't know?"

"Since you are my closest friend, I might as well tell you the whole truth." I paused for a moment before speaking again. "Technically, I married her to benefit me and Brenda, not because I loved her. Her father was my godfather, and he promised me one million dollars if I married his daughter." Samuel choked on the joint he was smoking and shook his head.

"So, you're telling me you got a Black Bill Gates as your godfather. Brenda, the secretary you just hired and got caught having sex with?"

"Yeah. Brenda is my main bitch, and two, she came to the job interview on her own. Kay was the cash cow for my two kids, Brenda, and me. If you expect me to say I feel guilty about it, I don't. I got the house I wanted, and the money to start my main hustle besides the church." Samuel had a confused look on his face.

"Damn, Charlie, you got a whole other life. I mean, it's still fucked up. We both know Kimberly really loves you. What kind of business? Selling weed?"

"I own a cannabis shop across town that Brenda and I opened several years ago." Samuel seemed too shocked to speak for a moment. "Are you okay, Samuel?" I asked.

"So, you're telling me you got another woman, kids, and you're selling weed. You're my friend and all, but you're full of surprises. Juicy taught you well, I see."

CHAPTER SIX
CHARLIE

I was still feeling salty about Kandi and her new lover boy. I knew it was best not to approach them, but I watched from a distance. When I got closer, I saw Kandi having sex with her lover facing the upstairs window. It was clear whose side she was on. I figured she was just another stripper, and I could always find another one. My phone rang, interrupting my thoughts, and it was Juicy. He wanted me to join him for some fishing so we could talk, which I found odd. When I arrived at the lake, he wasn't wearing his usual pimp outfit but looked like a black fisherman instead.

"You ready to start fishing, young blood?" he asked.

"Yeah. Why did you pick fishing? Wouldn't the bar have been better?"

"Too much noise. I think best in silence. Too many distractions."

"Whatever. There must be something you really want to talk about."

"You've been a hot topic lately," he said, taking several puffs of his joint and looking out at the water as if I wasn't even there. I wanted to walk away, but leaving him could be deadly.

"What do you mean?" I asked.

"You made the six o'clock news." He laughed.

"What's so funny? I don't see anything funny."

"You might want to join the unemployment line. I'm sure the church members won't be so forgiving. Got Sister Jenkins on TV talking about you embarrassing the church. You know she has ties with the government, right? And... Brenda?"

"You predicting I'm gonna get fired? The church adores me. Brenda ain't going anywhere. She made it very clear she's not going back to the poor house." Juicy laughed.

"Charlie, you've got tunnel vision. Remember, the church is a business, not a place for empathy. They may love you, but the people running the church don't care. I know what you did. Used marriage to make you two rich. You're not much different from me."

"Honestly, I don't care about the church firing me. Pretending to be a caring pastor isn't easy. And let me be very clear: I'm nothing like you." Juicy looked at me for a moment before speaking and took several more puffs of his joint.

"So, you're pretending to care about that boy?" I looked at him funny. He continued with a stern look.

"Think I don't know about that charity case of yours?" I stayed quiet and looked at him strangely.

"He reminds me of you when you were his age. Don't worry, I'm not going to introduce him to my line of work. He's a good kid. His mom used to work for me before she got pregnant with him. She was the one that got away," Juicy said.

"She was a whore like my mother?" I asked.

"Charlie, people change. Look, I know you have issues with your mom, but I won't let you degrade this one. Like I said, she turned her life around."

"Is that boy your son? You never defend a woman…"

"That's none of your concern. All I ask is don't give him a bad outlook on women. And keep those mommy issues to yourself or go sit on somebody's couch."

CHAPTER SEVEN
KIMBERLY

L ately, my nightmares have been intense, linked to me chasing Charlie down the street with his mistress in tow. Today was therapy day. I arrived at my therapist's session like usual when I saw two African figures on her shelf, which took me back to my childhood.

I was eight at the time and watching TV when I saw a commercial promoting self-love and natural hair. It made my face light up because I didn't see many commercials celebrating how I looked. "You think you're something, huh?" asked my momma. I looked at her with curiosity in my brown eyes.

"Momma, do we come from kings and queens?" She just looked at me as if I spoke Chinese.

"That's what people think. You would fit in just fine with those people."

"They look like my great-grandmother," I said.

"Listen, your great-grandmother was an uneducated housemaid, and nobody wanted her. Just like nobody wants you."

Shondra's tapping of her pen brought me back to the present.

"Nightmares again?" she asked. She looked at me with a questioning look, meaning there was more to the story besides the nightmares I was having.

" Kimberly, I know there's something you're not telling me."

"I had a nightmare where I found Sara lying in her bed, beaten to death, and Charlie was sitting in the room looking at her. He said he got the devil out of her. I screamed and woke up." She became quiet after that and took a piece of gum out of her pocket. That was unusual.

" Kimberly, you know life can sometimes foreshadow the future. It could mean your daughter Sara could be in danger. But do you love her?"

"I love her more than anything." I don't remember breaking down, but I remember crying in her arms. It was a way to release the frustrations I had.

" Kimberly, I get it. We deal with the trauma of seeing it almost every day on television and being black in America. But I must ask, what do you see when you look at Sara?"

"Honestly, I feel like I see myself. I see the big lips, big nose, and chocolate complexion which I grew up being told was ugly. Nonblack women like the Kardashians made the cloning of the black figure cool. It's like you drink diet coke instead of the real one. I spoke to my child as if my mother would take over. I would feel like shit afterward. When I read her diary, my heart broke, and I had a heart-to-heart conversation with her. I know I am her mother, but I am not an active mother."

"You haven't dealt with your mommy issues. You need to address them, or Sara will have the same issues when she grows up." She gets up and walks over to the floor mirror. I knew it meant one thing.

"My mom would never..."

"I want you to come over and look in this mirror. I want you to pretend that you are talking to your mother." I was reluctant at first, but I knew she wouldn't take no for an answer, so I gave in. I swallowed my pride and went over there. I took a deep breath and took a picture out of my pocket. Then I started talking.

"Why don't you love me? I didn't ask to be born. I remember you told me I would never amount to anything. Keyshawn was your golden child, and I was the child you wanted to hide away. All I wanted was a mother." She looked at the photo in my hand. I knew she wanted to know the backstory.

"It is the only picture I have of me sitting in her lap when I was five. She only did it because my grandma forced her to."

" Kimberly, how does that photo make you feel?"

"Like she saw me as a doll that she could throw to the side when she was done playing with me. I remember after the photo was taken, she left me on the couch and walked away. My grandmother came over to comfort me. Because my mother said, 'I'm done with that dark child,' as she walked away. I couldn't stop crying. It was as if a floodgate of childhood trauma was broken."

" Kimberly, you can stop this way of thinking with Sara. Black women have enough problems with the outside world. For example, I'm the best therapist, but I have to work twice as hard. There are times I have made appointments over the phone, and when they come in, they are displeased with my appearance. It was partially because my appearance didn't match the voice on the phone." She paused for a moment.

"You think I want to be my mother? I vowed to never become her."

"It doesn't matter what I think. What matters is what Sara thinks. She is seeing you the same way you saw your mother." I saw the face of my mother looking back at me.

"How's the OCD group session going?" the therapist asked. I wasn't in the mood to talk about that because sometimes going there made me feel like something was mentally wrong with me.

"It's fine." I went home to a house void of love. Charlie no longer came to dinner, and I no longer felt his touch. He would indirectly mention other women. Sometimes, I would wake up to find notes with foul names from an unknown source, but they were written by Charlie. My spirit was ripped from me, leaving me to feel like I was being controlled by my father.

"You're a worthless bitch." On top of that, Charlie left me on the floor without realizing the kitchen window was open. "I love you too, baby," Charlie replied. I was there for him, not her. My existence or this marriage did not matter to him.

All he saw was a live-in maid instead of his wife. I had seen one of the love letters and poems he wrote by accident, but I never received them. Our sex life died ten years ago, sad to say. What is wrong with me? I have been a loyal, damn near perfect wife, and he still walks away from me. I knew then he had no interest in me because of my looks. My bones reminded me every day I was no longer the young, vibrant woman I was. I was in my mid-thirties but felt Charlie was draining the life out of me, I thought to myself.

The following morning, Tianna and I were on the porch when breaking news came on her phone, which said Tyler Jones was killed because the police thought he was holding a gun when he was actually holding a water gun. He was only ten.

"I'm sick of this bullshit. How many times are we gonna get killed before they get the message? They just killed Breonna Taylor last week, and that one made me feel a certain way."

"Actually, I talked about it with my therapist." Tianna stopped smoking the joint in her hand and looked at me.

"You... seeing a therapist? Miss leaves everything in God's hands. How does your Pastor husband feel about that?"

"He does not know, and if he did, he would not care either way. Back to my point, we were talking about being black and a woman in America."

" Kimberly, it's a curse and a blessing to be black. Society don't give a fuck about black women. Do you know how many go missing every day? Don't tell me you think it's the white man holding us back. We hold ourselves back."

"I am not blaming the white man. I have white blood in me."

"Hell, we all do. Heard of the masters and the slaves without consent? Prime example is Thomas Jefferson."

"I know that, Kimberly, but my great-great-great-great-great uncle founded the town I was born in. He fell in love with a woman he saw in Africa and brought her over, and she became his maid and lover."

"That's all sweet and all, but that ain't nothing but bullshit. Interracial love wasn't a thing back then and wasn't widely accepted. I bet he was fucking her in the dark and parading around his wife in the daytime. How many half-breeds did they have?"

"TIANNA? You cannot say that word."

"It's a racial slur." Tianna looked at me.

"That's what my momma called them. How many did they have?"

"Six. I am not talking about it further."

"You're the one that brought it up. Remember? But what did the therapist say?"

"Nothing I didn't already know. Like the Kardashians, people wanting to be black."

"You know those bitches have manufactured bodies, which is the black body mode. Personally, nothing beats a natural-looking woman, and people who pretend to be black ain't meant to be black. I'm unique, and I got the features people pay to get. Yes, being a black woman in America ain't easy, but I wouldn't trade it for anything. You need to think the same way."

Tianna pulled out a joint and walked over to my wooden crates with vinyl discs inside it.

"You like that old shit, huh?" Tianna smirked. I was hoping she wasn't gonna find any of my opera music because i knew her ignorant ass would be asking me why I liked something so unusual. Personally, I would choose opera over the music that comes out today. "First of all, blues is the base of all music you hear today. Like Etta James, Nina Simone, and Chuck Berry. They are the pioneers that paved the way for us. Not Elvis Presley stealing shit and getting famous for it."

"Ok! I don't need the lecture. Nobody said it was trash. Give me some Nicki Minaj, Cardi B, Big Latto. Even Trina's old music. We got taste in two different eras. Let me ask though, what is y'all's song?"

Huh? I looked at her like she was crazy.

"Look Kimberly every couple has a song that's signature to them. For example, mine was Freak a leek with my ex. So, what's it for you two?" I ignored her question for several minutes, but she would not let me off the hook.

"I'm **waiting** for an answer," she said, impatiently.

"We have none," I muttered. Tianna coughed on the joint puff and almost dropped the joint in her hand.
"Ain't that a bitch! I bet he got a song with that secretary." She laughed.
"Why you have to bring *her* up?"

"Because I want to. You're in denial about that. He can cheat but you gotta stay home being the loyal wife. Trifling ass nigga."

"You sound just like Keyshawn," I said.

"Because we're right. Need to take off the blinders and see that." An hour later Tianna went back home, and I was so relieved.

CHAPTER EIGHT
KIMBERLY

Even though Tianna was my best friend, I didn't want her involved more than she already was in my marriage. I hopped into my run-down blue Beetle and left while Sara was asleep, and Charlie was nowhere to be found. I knew I would find Keyshawn outside in her garden. I nicknamed it the man-made jungle. There were a variety of flowers in colors, sizes, and names you'd usually find at Lowes. I assumed she never had kids, and the plants were her babies. Why else would you plant so many trees? To me, it was just a headache.

I found Keyshawn on all fours, inserting herself into those bushes like she was Tarzan talking to the plants. "Something might be really wrong with her," I thought. Keyshawn stood up, her pants stained with dirt like she'd been wrestling in mud all day, and her hair embedded with sticks, leaves, and branches. "What are you doing here? You didn't bring Sara with you?" she asked, coming near me with her dirt-covered hands that looked like bear paws with long, manicured nails that resembled claws.

"She's home." I knew Sara would never go near Keyshawn's garden; she was too much like me. Sara would hire people to do the hard labor. In my mind, there was nothing cute about a woman working in the garden.

"I've been thinking. Tianna and I had a conversation the other day."

"What does that have to do with me? We both know Tianna doesn't hold back."

"I know. The topic of Charlie came up." Keyshawn froze like a Popsicle and fled into the house as if afraid she'd melt in the sunlight. It was her way of avoiding something she didn't want to discuss. I thought maybe I had come by too early and disturbed her time with her plants.

"Keyshawn, why are you walking away from me?" I asked.

"Because when you come to my house this early, I know you want to involve me in Charlie's mess."

"You're right, but you're my partner in crime. Tianna can't keep a secret and would tell the whole neighborhood. You love seeing Charlie suffer. You hate his guts." Keyshawn grinned, knowing I was right. Revenge on Charlie would be sweet. She went to get some iced tea before returning to the living room.

"What do you want to find out about Charlie? His criminal background? His mysterious past? You married a stranger!" Keyshawn sipped her iced tea, her eyes saying, "You married that bastard."

"Keyshawn, stop! Tianna already chewed me out."

"Then you should've stayed home. You're in your feelings because you don't want to listen."

"Are you going to help or not?"

"Fine. How's therapy going?"

"Just *fine.*"

"Look, Kimberly, your husband does things without telling you. I saw him at the supermarket with another woman. They were acting like lovebirds." I was in denial about my husband entertaining other women in public or that we had drifted apart long before his new fling.

"I'm not stupid, Keyshawn! I know something is different." Keyshawn shook her head and headed back towards the kitchen, but this time she brought back a bottle of vodka. Alcohol always seemed to numb the pain in her mind.

" Kimberly, stop being a Debbie Downer. This should do the trick." Keyshawn put the vodka on the coffee table, grabbed her laptop, and flopped back down next to me.

"You come over here at 9 a.m. asking for help, and I'm helping. He's showing another woman around town like she's his wife. You've stayed with him for nearly two decades, and this is how he treats you. He's out being a playboy while you're locked up like a caged animal."

"Is this necessary?" Keyshawn's hands typed rapidly on her laptop. Her eyes widened for a moment before she slammed it shut and drank half the vodka bottle. She got quiet, avoiding eye contact.

"What's wrong, Keyshawn?" She kept biting her nails and chewing her bottom lip. It couldn't be that bad. It's not like he killed anyone. She left me on the couch and went to get another bottle of vodka and a jar, bringing them back to the living room. She slid them closer to me when she sat back down.

"Hate to tell you, but you're married to a ghost." Keyshawn tried to joke, but I wasn't in the mood. Ghosts didn't exist in my world, and the only ghost I knew was Casper. Charlie might not have been home much, but he wasn't a ghost; I thought he was the son of the devil instead.

"There are no ghosts in my house. Charlie isn't a ghost. You're spending too much time in that jungle of yours."

"It's not a jungle. It's a garden and a peaceful place for me. That has nothing to do with the fact he doesn't exist." Keyshawn threw her hands up, shoved the computer to me, and left for her garden. I couldn't believe what I was seeing. Charlie Garden was deceased. That was impossible. I walked out to Keyshawn, feeling I had been too harsh. She always beat around the bush instead of telling the truth.

"Sorry for not believing you, but stop beating around the bush. I can't believe he lied to me about everything. Who the hell am I married to?" Keyshawn dug her shovel into the soil, and I knew I was about to face her drama queen ego.

"Truthfully, I don't know how you don't believe it. You've got to be a piece of shit to take the identity of a dead person. You don't need a man to have a life." I knew Charlie lied, but I didn't want to jump to conclusions. Plenty of people have the same name. He could have his reasons. I wasn't going to call it quits because of this mind-blowing lie. Keisha always found excuses to say I should be single. What she said next went through one ear and out the other.

"Just because I'm alone doesn't mean I'm miserable. I'd rather be happy by myself. I'm not the one in a marriage based on lies. I don't need a man to be happy. Do you want to continue living in denial?"

"Keyshawn, I get the point. I just thought when we got married everything would be okay. But now I don't even know who I married." She might want to stop throwing darts and shut up. When she gets married, then she can give me advice. When I got back, Charlie was in his favorite spot on the couch.

From the look on his face, I knew he was mad about something.

"I need to talk to your mother." Sara left the room in a flash, fear on her face. But when I looked up, she was peeking from the top of the stairs. Charlie took out his vanilla-flavored cigar, crossed his legs, and stared at me. I went to get a drink from the kitchen, with him following like a bloodhound.

"I'm only gonna ask you once. Where were you this morning? I came home to find you gone and Sara asleep in her room."

"Charlie, I had something to do. What do you expect me to do? Stay in the house all night? I have things I want to do too!"

"Did you visit Keyshawn?"

"No. Why?"

"Every time you talk to Keyshawn, you grow some balls." Charlie's cell phone rang, and we looked at each other in silence. He grabbed the phone, still glaring at me. Minutes later, there was a knock at the door.

"Miss Grace?" I was relieved; he wouldn't lay a hand on me with Miss Grace there. She joined me in the kitchen. She never liked being in the living room with Charlie. I was making tea while she tapped her fingers on the table.

"Was I interrupting something? Charlie was sitting in there with a mad mug on his face." I knew Miss Grace saw and heard too much. She knew the true nature of my marriage, but I was glad she came.

"No."

"I'm going to the supermarket. Wanna come?"

"I gotta ask..." Miss Grace pulled me by my arm into the living room.

"Listen to me. Kimberly's coming to the supermarket with me, and you're not going to say or do anything about it. Lay a hand on her tonight, and I'll be waiting at your doorstep in the morning. I don't miss anything. Let's go!"

"But the tea?"

"I'm sure this idiot will get it. Unless he wants to be homeless." I was anxious about what would happen after I got back home. The ride to the supermarket was silent for a while. She finally spoke when she parked the car.

"What's really bothering you? You looked like a scared puppy in that kitchen." I looked away.

"Kim, I've been around long enough to know something isn't right. What happened before I came?"

"Charlie doesn't like that I talk to Keyshawn. Or that I haven't cut her off like he wants."

"Listen, I've got a sister that can be bitchy at times. I wish a man would tell me to cut her out of my life. The only reason to do that is if she's toxic and dangerous. But that's not the case."

"Well... Keyshawn is a lonely bitch."

"So what? She's your sister. I can bet a hundred dollars she'll be by your side before he would." It left me wondering.

CHAPTER NINE
KEYSHAWN

Kimberley got some nerve coming to bother me about her damn husband. I was glad when she left because I wasn't in the mood to deal with her bullshit. Just when I thought I would have a peaceful day, I was interrupted by Khandish.

"Hello," said Khandish.

"Why are you calling this early in the morning?"

"Has it crossed your mind that I just want to talk to my best friend? Can I come over, and we have a good old girl talk for the day, unless you're preoccupied with Terrell?"

"Terrell left for work early this morning. Just because he's around doesn't mean you can't come by to visit. Unless Terrell and I are..."

"Fucking. I **know**."

"You're already at my door, aren't you?" I asked.

"How do you know?" Khandish has a habit of calling my phone while parked outside my house. Just as I expected, she was parked outside.

"I see your car. Bring your ass in this house." Several minutes later, I heard her boots clomping through my door. She made a beeline for the cookies on my countertop, bypassing me to get to them. A few minutes later, she flopped down on my couch, and I gave her the side eye.

"So, what does Miss Goody Two Shoes want?" she asked.

"What are you talking about, Khandish?" I asked.

" Kimberly. She was over here, wasn't she?" I gave her a funny look, wondering how long she had been sitting outside my house.

"You sat outside and waited until she left, didn't you? And why do you call her that?" Khandish folded her arms, rolled her eyes, and looked at me.

"It ain't a secret I don't fuck with Kimberly. I call her that because she always acts like she does everything by the rules. Yet her ass is down at the strip club shaking it." I was mind-blown by what she just said because that was the last place I expected Kimberly to be.

"Khandish, is this one of your jokes? Kimberly barely wears a two-piece bathing suit on the beach. Being naked in front of strangers doesn't seem like something she would do. Maybe it's someone who looks like her."

"Does this face look like I'm joking? I know how your sister looks, and I saw her firsthand."

"Did she see you?" I asked.

"It's dark in there, and strippers can't see the crowd from the stage. You sure she ain't turned to women? I mean, we both know Charlie ain't fucking her."

" Kimberly isn't into women. I got a feeling you are salty about her because you might want her." Khandish had a disgusted look on her face.

"I got a type, and your sister ain't one of them."

"You like those redbones." Khandish couldn't keep from grinning.

"We both got our weaknesses. So yes, mine is redbones, and yours is that dick that belongs to Terrell." She paused for a moment before speaking again. "What's the deal with Donovan? My cousin was flirtatious with him, and he pretended like she wasn't even standing there."

"Donovan only has eyes for one girl."

"Let me guess. It's Kimberly."

"Between you and me, Kimberly should've married Donovan instead. Nobody knows this, including Kimberly, but she cried herself to sleep for months after Donovan left for college. She even slept with his varsity jacket."

"Why doesn't she divorce that no-good husband of hers then?"

"She doesn't believe in divorce. 'Till death do us part' is instilled in her brain. She feels that Donovan threw her to the wayside."

"Fuck that shit. She needs to go get what makes her moan at night."

"Khandish!"

"Don't be yelling at me because it's the truth. It's the same thing as when you were married to that jackass, but we both knew you really wanted Terrell. You only married him because he was good on paper. Speaking of that jackass, when are you gonna tell your sister why you hid from the world for six years and about your ex-husband?"

"Why? She's hard-headed and stubborn. She'll never listen to me."

"Personally, I wouldn't tell her anything, but you should because you're the only sane family member she has. She also needs to know you can relate to her situation."

"So you're Dr. Phil *now*?"

"It's my opinion, and sometimes your ass doesn't want to listen either. *Must run in the family*."

CHAPTER TEN
CHARLIE

P inkey was the bar/strip club I would go to ease my mind. It always had a special place in my heart. It was where I came with my uncle and where I lost my virginity. Cardi B's "Money" was blasting through the speakers. Samuel needed to get out of his funk, so we decided to go to the downtown bar. He was my alibi and excuse to go. Once we got there, Samuel zoned in on a girl at a table. She was apple butter brown with dark freckles, brown eyes, and pink cupid-shaped lips.

"I'mma go…"

"Go ahead, Samuel." He always got weak between the legs when it came to brown-skinned women. I was at the strip club to get some drinks and watch Kandi dance. She had three days to obey, or she would face the consequences. The bar's interior was dark brown wood, nearly midnight black, with smoke swirling around like clouds. The floor creaked like it was in pain whenever someone walked on it.

As I was minding my business, an elderly man took the stool next to me. He reminded me of my great uncle Greg, who drank whiskey every Saturday and Sunday. But this old man reeked of a blue-collar worker who never made time for others. He had kinky, coarse grey hair, one ocean-blue eye, and one dark brown. Smoking had aged him, making his skin look like crumbling clay. Thin pink lips and eyes that stuck out like a crackhead on cocaine. Dressed like one of those black golf club members.

"Down on your luck, young man?" he asked in a German accent. "Women driving you crazy?" He chuckled.

"You don't know the half of it." I sighed. He took several gulps of his Bud Light before speaking again.

"Think I got this grey hair for nothing? So, what's on your mind? Did your wife kick you out?" I didn't have to answer because he answered for me with his eyes, but another customer chimed in.

"Oh, wife problems?" said another customer sitting next to me. He looked like a life-sized lumberjack with orange hair like Prince Harry and unusually grey eyes. The older man gave him a scolding look.

"Like I was saying, I've had several of those during my lifetime." He slid his beer glass to the bartender, mouthing for another drink. "My first was my high school sweetheart, but we were kids and grew apart."

"Here's your drink, Bob," said the bartender.

"Thanks." The older man chuckled. "The last three seemed like they were from hell..." He laughed. I tuned out his rambling when I saw Kandi dancing on the stage.

"That's a nice piece of ass," said a customer.

"She's off limits," I replied. He looked at me while finishing his drink. Once done, he faced me.

"How you gonna claim a stripper? You got wife problems, remember?" The older man shook his head before taking another sip of his drink.

"Wasn't nobody talking to you," I said.

"Well, I can't help but overhear the conversation."

"Shut your fat ass up and keep your opinions to yourself. You're the last person to talk. Your bitch almost cut off your penis." He drank his beer in silence after that. I wasn't going to take any bullshit from this drunk.

"My household ain't none of your business. The one on stage is off limits." The older gentleman gave me a strange look.

"You the pimp? Butch has a point. Ain't no name tag on her! I don't like no damn pimp, and my son turned into one." I let them talk and finished my drink.

"I ain't no pimp. Women ain't nothing but property and baby-making machines."

"Sounds a bit harsh," the older man said, putting down his beer. "I may have hated my wives, but I would never say that about them."

"Look, mister, you don't know my wife. I think it's time I left," I angrily replied.

"Be careful what you wish for. Every decision you make comes with consequences..." the older man

77

said as I got up and left the bar. I figured Samuel would find his way back home.

CHAPTER ELLEVEN
CHARLIE

People say nobody can drive you to look at other women or cheat. But I disagree. I wasn't thrilled about the marriage, but I was excited about someone cooking and cleaning with me. I remember the day I got married. I was glad Kandi called, so I excused myself from Kay and the old white bitch. I met Kandi at the strip club one night after an argument with Kay. I was having a drink with one of my buddies, a regular named Benjamin.

He had the same syndrome as me: "Nagging wives." This was my second time at this strip club. I used to go to the one across town, but one of the strippers' pimps didn't like that I was interested in his property. The strip club was slightly dark with neon lights. Cardi B's "She Bad" played over the stereo. It was filled with a variety of shades of melanin, ranging from sizes 0 to 22, but one caught my eye.

"I see you eyeing the new girl," said Benjamin. She was on stage performing, and I couldn't keep my eyes off her. "I call her Sweetness," Benjamin said, but she reminded me of Kandi. She had an exotic look, an hourglass body, and a complexion like thick molasses. She wore a pink bra and thong that popped against her skin. Afterward, she came over to us. Benjamin's face beamed as if she was coming over to him, but I knew she had her eyes on me.

"I see you like what you see," she purred.

"I do," replied Benjamin.

"I was talking about your friend here." Benjamin's face went blank while mine lit up.

"You're Cassie's client or John or whatever. You ain't my type." I knew that was my cue to talk.

"You remind me of a chocolate candy bar. Do you mind if I call you Kandi?"

"Not at all. My clients all have their nicknames for me. I prefer yours. What should I call you?"

"My wife calls me Charlie." I saw her side-eye me when she looked down at my wedding ring finger, which had a faint discoloration around it.

"Should've known you were one of those types." Benjamin chuckled next to me.

"*Types*?"

"Married ones. I've had my share of those." She sat on my lap with her hand on my crotch. It was the first time I noticed Kandi's almond-shaped, brownie-chocolate-colored eyes. She had kissable lips that made me smile because I had naughty thoughts.

"Is it a problem?"

"Nah, I want your money, not a relationship with you." Kandi may have told me she didn't want a man, but she couldn't ignore my interest. Here we are ten months later, and now she's my mistress, which I wanted in the first place.

"You still with the 'fat cow' you call a wife? What about your daughter? Do you even have a relationship with her?" Kandi ranted on the phone.

"I don't care about that cow! I can't afford a divorce. The kid has none of my DNA!" My parents had been bugging me about having grandchildren. They knew her body couldn't handle it due to her miscarriages.

Kay thinks I don't know who her baby daddy is. Twelve years ago, on a March spring day, Kay and I were having one of our arguments, and I left her ass at the gas station. I should've known her ass wasn't loyal then. I came back to get her dumb ass, and she jumped in the truck with some random motherfucker as if she didn't care about me. She had the nerve to get pregnant by him. Playing the gentleman, I accepted her and that damn bastard baby. Kay just needs to focus on keeping the house clean and having my meals ready when I come home. All Kandi needed to believe was that Kay was being a whore and stepped out on me and got pregnant. Kandi's voice brought me back to the present.

"Tell her the truth!" Kandi replied. "Do you even love the child?"

"Not really." I changed the subject. "Where do you want to meet me?"

"The coffee shop downtown," she replied.

"I can't wait." I knew Kay had been listening the entire time. She heard parts of what was being said, but from the sweet tone of my voice, she knew it was a woman. It had been years since I spoke to her kindly or sweetly. The first year of marriage, it seemed we had sex 24/7. I talked sweetly to her constantly. Now, even the way I looked at her had changed. At one time, my eyes were full of love for her; now, my eyes were full of disgust and resentment. Instead of growing old together, it had turned into a nightmare. She was a burden. She interrupted my conversation.

"Who was that on the phone? Somebody from work? Family member? Who!" she demanded as I continued to ignore her. "You prefer to talk to them instead of your wife? Do you even care about what I have to say? Apparently, whoever is on the phone is more important than me or how I feel."

"I will call you later," I finally said as I hung up the phone.

By now, Kay was furious. "What is your problem? You never talk to me that way anymore. Must be your grandmother."

"Yeah," I lied. "It was my grandmother." She knew by my cold response I was not being truthful. My maternal grandmother was long dead. My paternal grandmother was deaf.

"It is a shame you have your grandmother fooled. You cannot toy with people's emotions. Not everyone is as tolerant as me or looks the other way. I still love you, but you fail to realize that," Kay said. I was on the verge of giving Kay a black eye if she didn't stop talking.

"Kay, if you stopped nagging me all the time, maybe you would see a different side of me," I responded.

"I should not have to nag you. For the record, I am not a bitch. I am your wife, not your girlfriend. We go 50/50 on everything. I have been there for you."

"Don't need to or want to hear that sentimental bullshit. You're my wife. I could've traded you for a trophy wife." I laughed.

"Why are you so cruel, Charlie?" Kay cried.

"I ain't being cruel; you never liked the truth. I need to go for a ride to clear my head. I won't be home for dinner," I spoke.

"Go on then, Charlie. Your negative energy is a poison around here."

"Shut the fuck up!" I yelled.

Kay went to the kitchen, returning with a knife. "If you ever tell me to shut up again, you will see heaven sooner than you thought." She screamed at me. "Who is she?"

"Kay, you're losing it. What are you talking about?" She threw a tube of lipstick at me.

"I am not dumb! I see that damn fuchsia lipstick on your collar. So, I am gonna ask you again, who is she? Quite frankly, I cannot believe you would do that to me. Don't I make your ungrateful ass happy? Huh?"

"Where did you get that from?"

"I should be asking you the same question. I do not wear this color. I am a curvy brown melanin woman who has been down for you. You got some trashy woman in this relationship."

"Kay, you found that outside and are trying to pin it on me. Only strippers wear that color."

"But you let her kiss you. I dedicated my life to this marriage, and you..." All I heard was blah, blah, blah, with her waving the knife at me.

"What's your damn problem? Let the shit go!"

"Let it go?" My cell phone went off, which I thought I could use as an excuse to get away. Inside, she kept coming at me with the knife. So, her ass got what she deserved when I took the knife from Kay and pushed her against the wall.

I walked out the door, leaving Kay on the floor with the knife in her hand. There was an aroma of burned meat with water overflowing from a pot, but I was disconnected from the mess or Kay. She always wore white maxi dresses because they used to make me happy. I left Kay balled up on the floor with a broken glass vase and her favorite white maxi dress ripped to pieces.

CHAPTER TWELVE
KIMBERLY

A s I woke up, I noticed an empty spot in the bed, which wasn't unusual. However, there was an 8x11 inch sheet of notebook paper with red ink on it, and a black rose beside it. Charlie always wrote with the colors of his emotions. When he was angry, he used red; blue when he was feeling down; purple, green, etc., when he was unwell. To be honest, I don't know what color he used when he was happy because I hadn't seen that emotion in years. The way Charlie wrote was also a giveaway to what he was thinking. His handwriting was neat when he was angry but turned to chicken scratch when he wasn't feeling well. I picked up the note which said:

DEAR YOU (WIFE),

I AM GOING TO BE ON A BUSINESS TRIP FOR A COUPLE MORE DAYS. WHICH ALSO MEANS DON'T

THINK ABOUT RUNNING AWAY BECAUSE I HAVE EYES EVERYWHERE. I KNOW YOU'LL BE A TRAMP WHILE I'M GONE BECAUSE YOU'LL OPEN YOUR LEGS TO ANYONE. IF YOU WANNA BE A TRAMP IT BETTER NOT BE IN MY BEDROOM, AND IF I CATCH YOU WITH ANOTHER MAN, YOU'LL BE PUNISHED LIKE THE GIRL FROM THE 12 YEARS A SLAVE MOVIE. KEEP THAT NOSY BITCH ACROSS THE STREET OUT OF MY HOUSE ALONG WITH YOUR SISTER. YOU ALWAYS CHANGE WHEN THEY COME AROUND.

FROM HUSBAND

P.S.
DON'T BOTHER ME. I WON'T ANSWER THE PHONE.

I was glad he was gone so I could have a peaceful day without Charlie around. I threw the bed covers off, slipped on my oversized brown dog slippers, and played my favorite blues song as I got undressed to shower. The water against my body made me feel like the negative energy was being washed away. I never felt completely comfortable in my own house. Afterwards, I got dressed and went outside to my raggedy blue Beetle, which I'd had since the 90s. I had begged Charlie for a new car because this one had rust holes in the floor, torn seats, and faded paint, but he always said it wasn't in the budget. Even though I gave him my library paycheck, I couldn't get a new vehicle. That was messed up. Anyway, I had to go to Walmart because Charlie left no food in the house. I drove about five miles before the check engine light came on, which wasn't uncommon. But this time, there was an unusual sound I hadn't heard before.

"Clunk!" I thought I could call Charlie to send a tow truck since he had all the credit cards, but I should have known better. This is what happened when I called him.

"Hello?" That sneaky bitch had the nerve to answer his phone. Several minutes went by before he came on.

"What, Kay?" I sensed someone else was in the room, but I didn't care. I wanted him to be my husband and help me like a husband should.

"Look, you know I don't call unless I have to. My car broke down, and I need you to call a tow truck because you have the credit cards." There was silence on the other end, making me think he had already hung up.

"Kay, I don't have time for this nonsense. It's not my fault you didn't get rid of that junk car. Find your own way! Clunk!" Disbelief washed over me, but I shouldn't have been shocked. I sat there, unsure of what to do, until I saw Miss Grace's red Mustang coming down the road, blasting country music. She parked and came over to me.

"What's wrong with that junk car you got? I don't see any flat tires."

"My car broke down." I knew by her reaction that she already knew Charlie wasn't coming. She pushed me aside, popped the hood, and white smoke came streaming out. Her silence told me my beloved car was dead.

"Where are you heading? You're not gonna make it in this car. I can give you a lift."

"Walmart. If it's not interrupting anything?"

"Kim, whatever it is can wait. I'm not gonna let you walk several miles because your jackass husband took the car. You may not be blood, but you're kinfolk to me. Now, the same can't be said about Charlie." My own mother would have made me walk, like when I was pregnant, and she refused to take me without gas money. Once I got in the car, Miss Grace started blasting Blake Shelton. Don't get it twisted; I don't mind some country music, but some of it drives me crazy. I didn't dare touch the radio because last time she smacked my hand away.

Miss Grace had a tendency for road rage. Prime example: we were in the parking lot, and an old man had trouble parking in front of us.

"Non-driving fool! Getting on my nerves! Some folks shouldn't be driving." Everything else was fine until we got to the produce department, and she caught sight of something. Sometimes I think Miss Grace has eyes in the back of her head.

"What's wrong?" She ignored my question, but when I looked in the direction of her gaze, I understood.

"Bless her heart. Goodness gracious! She's got platinum blonde box braids, tar black complexion, hot bubblegum pink shorts up her ass. And her stomach is spilling out of her tank top like the Pillsbury Doughboy. Women walking around wearing crayon box colors on their heads, thinking they look cute. I hate to see how that face looks."

The woman turned around, reminding me of Rasputia Latimore from the movie "Norbit." When she came over to the produce section, she rolled her eyes at us.

"Ragamuffin." Miss Grace tasted several grapes before speaking again. She never said one sentence without another paragraph following.

"Don't be in public looking like that! EVER! Understand me? People have social media now, which means you'll be a trending topic."

"Yes, I understand, Miss Grace." Miss Grace and I looked at each other and chuckled.

"You young'uns are something else. But I love you like my own. I gotta ask, why do you always wear white? You know there are other colors in the rainbow. Like that actress Lupita. She's your complexion and can wear any color."

"Charlie says I look best in white. It reminds him of an angel statue."

"Kim, you're not a damn statue! He's got you looking like a slave. Your house already looks like it belongs on a plantation."

"Really, Miss Grace? That doesn't sound right coming from you."

"Kim, I don't care how it sounds. You need to hear some hard truths. No woman walks around looking like you do unless she's a house slave."

"What the hell are you trying to say? This conversation is pointless." Before I could blink, she slapped me, leaving a red mark on my face. I looked at her in bewilderment.

"Who are you talking to? Little girl, I'll whoop your ass for speaking to me like that. If your hard head would listen, I'm trying to tell you something. I've been on this earth longer than you and gained wisdom along the way. So, you'd better take the advice I'm about to give you." Honestly, I wasn't in the mood to hear what she had to say after she slapped me, but she kept talking anyway.

"Kim, a marriage shouldn't be one-sided. If all you do is give everything to your husband and neglect your self-care, you will lose yourself and your identity. Look, I know you go to some group meetings and see a therapist..."

"How do you know? Tianna told you, didn't she? That girl can never keep her mouth shut," I said.

"KIM! Calm down. Tianna didn't tell me anything. I saw the brochure and therapist card on your table. I don't tell folks' personal business. There's nothing wrong with talking to people. It doesn't make you crazy. Take it from this old woman. I've had my share of bad seeds. I've been married multiple times. One was a hobosexual, the second a womanizer, the third an addict, and the fourth toxic. That last one had me in jail for breaking all the windows out of his car. After that, I knew I needed self-care. I don't want you going down the same path. Do something that makes you happy for once and not what he orders you to do."

After Miss Grace dropped me off, I went to my bedroom, put on some jazz, and fell asleep thinking about what she said.

CHAPTER THIRTEEN
CHARLIE

After writing that note to Kay, I was headed back to where my heart truly was. I put on my radio and played "All My Life" by J. Cole and Lil Durk. Ten minutes later, I arrived and saw my daughters racing out to my car.

"Daddy! Daddy!" Imani reached my car first, with Emily right behind her.

"There go my girls," I said, hugging them. Brenda came out of the house with her arms folded, clearly with something on her mind. Inside, I sat down at the island in the kitchen while the girls played in the living room. The moment Brenda grabbed a glass of wine and came back to face me, I knew something was on her mind.

"So, when are you gonna drop this married Pastor act?" Honestly, I didn't have an end in sight. I wanted my cake and to eat it too. I got a high off from the congregation praising me.

"Brenda..." She started pouring more wine into her empty glass before speaking again.

"Charlie, I've sat back and let you do you. But you ain't got much longer until I'm done with this shit."

"Watch your mouth! The girls can hear you." Brenda yelled for the girls to go to their rooms, and when they were gone, she turned her attention back to me.

"Now they're gone. Cut to the bullshit." She took another sip of her wine. "You think I like telling the girls you're on a damn business trip whenever you leave? Or knowing you married a woman you don't love but never thought about marrying me? Really?" Brenda was acting brand new, as if she didn't agree to this arrangement and now was mad despite getting all the benefits.

"Really? I did it for us. I don't see you complaining about what we got out of it. You act like I held a gun to your head and made you do it."

"You know damn well I wouldn't let my children grow up in poverty. Yes, I enjoy what we have, but that doesn't change the fact you're gone nearly half the month and I sleep alone at night." Brenda turned away from me, and I knew it must've hit a nerve because she never turned away. I went over to where she was standing.

"Baby, I know it must be hard, especially for you, with me not being there. But I can't have you and my baby needing anything. That means by any means possible. I don't like doing this either, but it has to be done. Give me one more year, and I'm **done**."

CHAPTER FOURTEEN
KIMBERLY

As I stood at the door of the gas station, I couldn't shake the feeling that things were about to go sideways. I had no intention of getting caught, but bringing a junkie along was a mistake. When the situation turned chaotic, I had to take control. Killing the crackhead was my only option, and I threatened the cashier to keep quiet.

CHAPTER FIFTHTEEN
KIMBERLY

The following day I arrived at the library, and I saw the movie "What's love got to do with it" playing in the back room? I started thinking about my own life. Before I married Charlie, I thought that I would never see myself on television. While I was doing some computer work, I heard a male and female arguing outside. With me being nosy I went outside and found a male who was a middle-aged man with black wire like chest hair, oversized sunglasses, and spray tan complexion. The girl on the other hand looked like an overgrown little girl with her two blonde ponytails, two pink bows, two gumball brown eyes and up and down flat like a board.

"You think you can avoid my phone calls!?" The man roughly said.

"I don't have a phone attached to my hip 24/7," the woman said. I was looking at them with disgust on my face. As I was watching them one of my coworkers came up behind me. She was only sixteen but looked a good twenty-five with jet black hair and freckles that covered her face.

"That is shame," I said. My coworker popped her blueberry gum near my face and stood looking at me with a twisted face.

"What is with the face," I asked. She cut her eyes at me. I knew she was itching to say what she wanted to say. Like clockwork after she popped that damn bubble gum, she opened her mouth.

"Look, who's talking! Can't see the reflection looking back at you. Remember when your husband would be waiting outside for you when you got off. Police were called because you two were fighting and almost killed you." I was just about to go back inside when I heard a voice behind me.

"Kimmie?" My legs were glued to the ground for a moment. My co-worker could not keep her eyes off him.

"You know him," she asked me. I thought it was best not to say shit to her. But I could not forget Donovan. He had gone off to college on the west coast, which had been ten years since I last saw him. For some reason people felt sorry for him while others thought he was just another thug portrayed on TV media. If that meant being tough on his younger brother, so be it. He was the kid everybody felt sorry for, or others thought he was a lost cause. I looked at him and walked back in the library. Several minutes later I was at the checkout desk, and he came over to me.

"You really going to not speak to me. He let you work here?"

"What are you doing here? When was the last time you read a book?"

"I came back home because my mother got sick and my brother was running around wanting to be a wannabe thug. He bumps heads with Pops a lot." Butterflies started to form in my stomach with a warm feeling on the inside. I forgot how handsome he was. He had smooth dark chocolate complexion skin, baby blue eyes, 6ft tall, pearly white teeth, short haircut and Usher cologne on. Even though we grew up as friends I always had a soft spot for him.

"Is she better?"

"Who?"

"Your mother."

"She's good. I came over to talk to you, not my dysfunctional family. We should have married each other Kimmie, we make a good couple," he said under his breath.

"Sir, we ain't all day and I don't give a fuck about your broken heart," said another customer named Peaches. Had the nerve to think she looks good when she looks like an orange Fanta soda bottle. She always had something to say that did not warrant her opinion. When I left to go home Donovan was outside waiting for me.

"Donovan! What the fuck?" I forgot that he poked his lips out whenever he wanted to prove a point. His luscious lips made me think of an X-rated film and what he could do with that thick tongue of his. He pulled me in his embrace with his lip's inches away from mine.

"Kimmie you are not gonna give me the cold shoulder. Remember senior year of high school behind the gym bleachers. Let me give you a ride home."

"You just want what you cannot have. "The softness of his lips against my neck made me shiver.

"Kimmie, you don't know your own husband. Word on the street is that he got plenty of women. Kimmie, the only person that thinks Charlie is a saint is your mother." I snapped out his spell because nobody was gonna bad mouth my husband.

"Charlie may be a lot of things, but he will never cheat on me. We love each other."

"Really? Who were you thinking about when you were in my embrace? Him or what we can be? It was a setup!"

"Say what Donovan? What do you mean setup?" Donovan looked towards the wall before he spoke again. "The same night you met Charlie was the same night I wanted to talk to you..." Before he could finish his sentence, Tianna drove up.

"Kimberly?"

"That is my ride." I knew Tianna would ask questions and the moment I entered the car she was 21 questions shit.

"Is that Donovan? That's one fine piece of specimen of a man."

"Yes. How you know him?" A smirk came onto her face which meant one thing on her mind.

"You," she shot back at me.

"My childhood friend. So how do you know him?"

"Childhood friend? Ok. Almost locking lips with a childhood friend. You never thought about riding that dick?" She paused for a moment and looked at me. I looked away from her. "Or you already did. So, you know what I'm talking about. Everybody knows Charlie is a cheater. Should have fun on your own. Let's just say he and I had some fun back in the day." Had the nerve to cut her eyes at me. Smoked several puffs in my direction. Tiana was always thinking about sex. She is a free spirit and was not ready to settle down.

"That man got eyes for nobody, but you are now. I can be butt ass naked and he won't take the bait, but he'll look. All niggas do."

"Like you wearing that yellow bodycon dress? Friend my ass! This joint got you thinking delusional.

I see that twinkle in your eyes and it ain't for your husband. Donovan is a fine ass nigga. I bet he got a bigger dick than Charlie. Girl, I would buy a dildo if I was you and pretend it was his. We both a size queen diva."

"TIANA! I am married. Sex toys are unholy."

"Loyal to a man that pays you dust. Who you know has a roaming eye in the church? He does not look at you in the crowd when he does his sermon. Doesn't need a bunch woman around him and brag about his sex game. A real nigga knows how to make you wet by looking at you without saying a word. I ain't gonna stop asking." She looked at me.

" Kimberly, you gotta get out more often. See the world. Charlie doesn't take you nowhere. Probably through TV and books. Unholy? Really Kimberly? If it wasn't meant to be made God wouldn't allow it to be created. Charlie doesn't give a damn about being holy. Stop being a prune."

"Tiana you could do some reading yourself. Learn some things. Change the subject Tiana. You do not want me to talk about what you do. I see men…"

"Think I'm a dumb bitch or something. Let me set the record straight. I ain't selling ass to get money. I don't get to read books to know shit. I got something to show you." Tiana lit up another joint at my dinner table like I wasn't sitting next to her. Against better judgement I followed her to her house. I knew something was off when weed tickled my nose as I walked down her cellar. What the hell was she doing down here? Just like I suspected it was a weed laboratory.

"Tiana, what the hell you doing down here? This shit is illegal," I said.

"Look, I ain't got nothing to worry about. Nobody knows except you. U don't need a degree to run a profitable business. Before you ask, I'm the one that supplies Mr. Rogers with his weed, and I get a percentage of what he sold." I cannot believe this. She is the queen in charge the entire time.

"Have you two…."

"Hell, no Kimberly! We have a business relationship. I have other male friends for that. Mr. Rogers is the kind of old that don't make my panties wet." I had enough of this weed lab and walked back to my house with Tiana trailing behind me like a little puppy. I went into the kitchen and when I turned back around, she had the nerve to have her feet on my table and joint in her hand.

"Really? At my table?"

"I always smoke a joint when I hear a story about a handsome man. I want all the details and start from the beginning." I looked at her.

"What? Don't give me some half ass story. I'll admit I'm a nosy person and very visual."

"Whatever! Donovan and Terrell...."

"Girl, that brother of his is a fine ass nigga as well. Wouldn't mind being in the dark alone with...." She stopped midway through eating. "My bad continue with the story."

"Like I was saying Donovan, Terrell and I went to school together. Just to let you know Terrell has a thing for Keyshawn."

"Damn! I ain't interested in talking about Terrell. Let me get straight to the bullshit. Why are you acting liking you only fucked Donovan one time? Did you fuck him twelve years ago?"

"Why did you say post twelve years ago?"

"Have you looked at Sara and Donovan together? You and I both know two chocolate people can make a chocolate baby. But a light person and chocolate person wouldn't have a chocolate looking baby. Don't worry, I'm not going to tell everybody. It's safe for me. But I wanna know the history you have with Donovan."

"In high school. "Donovan and I were best friends but in ninth grade we took it a step further. Had real intercourse in tenth grade and did not stop until he left for college. What is a size queen diva?"

"Women who likes big dicks. But you ain't going to elaborate," she asked. "You got a husband, and you don't want him. Don't be mad when another woman grabs him and shows you what you could've had."

I revisited my love affair with vodka whenever I wanted to calm my nerves. It had been several months since I drank from the crystal-clear bottle that could be mistaken for water. Several hours Charlie arrived home with the scent of rose petals on his clothes.

"You drinking wine Kay? Normally your ass would be drinking whiskey or vodka." I was full flush drunk when he entered the living room. I had my legs scrambled over the couch with a vodka half full, eyes red from either the drinking, crying or both.

"Thinking about some...things."

"It's Keyshawn? I told you about talking to her. She ain't nothing but a hater for marriage."

"She is ....my sister." Charlie's demeanor became rigid and cold. Keyshawn was the only ally I had and blood other than my parents.

"Should that mean anything to me? She's always stirring up trouble. Banned from MY house."

"She...family." Charlie started pacing the floor back and forth. He stopped and looked me dead in the face.

"She's banned from my house for good!"

"NO!" Charlie pulled the vodka bottle out of my hand slapping me at the same time.

"Momma, how come you never smile? Miss Grace said some people can't smile."

"Sara don't pay her no mind. I do smile. Seeing you wake up in the morning and coming into the kitchen makes me smile." As we headed to the park Sara decided to turn on the radio to MEG Stallion new song.

"Throat bab......" That shit immediately got turned off.

"What the hell is that?"

"It's what you call music momma!" This little girl had gone and lost her mind talking to me like that.

"That ain't music! Talking explicitly about sex and your only twelve."

"And?" Her smart ass had the nerve to get an attitude. I made a quick U-turn and headed back towards the house when her demeanor completely changed. While I was taking a shower all I thought about was Donovan, but Charlie interrupted my thoughts.

"I'm going out of town." I thought he meant tomorrow but he was gone when I got out of the shower. I needed to talk to someone, but Miss Grace was gone. So, I called Donovan.

"Hello," said Donovan. His silky voice always made my heart skip a beat.

"Hey, Donovan!"

"Kimmie?"

"You busy?" I heard noises in the background and the faint sound of a woman's voice.

"Nah. What's up?"

"Is that a female I hear in the background?" Donovan chuckled.

"Cousin Kerry." Donovan laughed.

"You think it's a girl from a one-night stand?"

"Whatever! Can I get a ride to the store?" It got quiet on the other end for a moment and thought he had hung up. "Donovan?"

"No problem. Where's your husband? Lemme guess away on business." I thought it was best not to answer the question and he read between the lines.

"When?"

"Now? I mean if you got nothing else to do."

"I'll be there in an hour." My stomach was filled with butterflies and my heart was beating like a drum. I ran into my closet to find my yellow body hugging bodycon dress. I knew this was not a date, but I did not want him to think I was homely. He showed up like he said looking like a delicious chocolate candy bar.

"Hey, Kimmie! He told you he's going away on business huh?" Donovan smirked, folded his arms, and rolled his eyes.

"Do not give me that look," I remarked. He went over to sit on the couch. Within seconds later Sara came running downstairs. The moment I saw them together I knew who she truly looked like. It was as if they had known each other since her birth.

"Only one huh? You can pretend if you want. But I gotta be real with you." He pauses for a moment.

"When were you going to tell me?" I knew the conversation would come up once he saw her.

"Donovan…."

"Tell me the truth **KIMBERLY**!"

"I got pregnant from the night you picked up from the gas station." I honestly thought when Donovan moved away, he would never come back. Now I realize it was a decision not to tell him came back to bite me in the ass.

"Kimmy, you really think I would abandon my child?" The rest of the time was a blur and didn't say anything when he dropped me off…

This concludes BOOK ONE in the "Why Doesn't He Love Me," series. Find out what happens next in the following installment "Why Doesn't He Love Me: Book Two" available for purchase online.